ID605399

CHOCOLATE TREE

A
MAYAN
FOLKTALE

LINDA LOWERY
AND
RICHARD KEEP

ILLUSTRATED BY
JANICE LEE PORTER

On My Own
FOLKLORE

M Millbrook Press/Minneapolis

Millbrook Press
A division of Lerner Publishing Group, Inc.
241 First Avenue North
Minneapolis, MN 55401 U.S.A.

Website address: www.lernerbooks.com

Library of Congress Cataloging-in-Publication Data

Lowery, Linda, 1949–
      The chocolate tree : a Mayan folktale / adapted by Linda Lowery and Richard Keep;
   illustrations by Janice Lee Porter.
         p. cm. — (On my own folklore)
      ISBN 978-0-8225-7545-0 (lib. bdg. : alk. paper)
      1. Mayas—Folklore. 2. Chocolate—Folklore. 3. Mexico—Folklore. I. Keep, Richard
   Cleminson. II. Porter, Janice Lee, ill. III. Title.
   F1435.3.F6L68 2009
   398.2'0899742—dc22   2007001648

Manufactured in the United States of America
1 2 3 4 5 6 – DP – 14 13 12 11 10 09

*big chocolate-covered hugs to
Caleb, Cody, Ava, Elaine, Caroline, and Lydia
—L.L. and R.K.*

*to Cynthia Schildhauer, artist and friend
—J.L.P.*

The Jungle Kingdom

Chocolate ice cream.

Warm cocoa.

Fudge brownies.

Can you imagine a world

without chocolate?

This is a folktale about how

chocolate came to all of us on Earth.

It begins nearly 1,000 years ago

in a rain forest in Mexico.

Among the chattering parrots
and huge butterflies,
there lived a special group of people.
They were called the Maya.
The Maya grew trees full of fruit.
They had bees that gave them honey.
But they did not have chocolate.
Mayan farmers worked
on farms called milpas.
They grew beans and squash
and sweet potatoes.
They grew maize, a type of corn.
How did these crops get to Mexico?
Well, that's an interesting part
of the Mayan story.
They came from paradise!

A king named Kukulkán
carried seeds for the crops
all the way to Earth from
his home in paradise.
Like the bird called the quetzal,
he wore a cloak of colorful feathers.

He looked like a man-size bird.
His skin glistened in the sun
like a jungle snake's.
So he looked like a serpent too.
This made him mysterious
and beautiful.

He was not just a king.

He was also a god.

Paradise was home to all the gods.

But Kukulkán spent most of his time
on Earth.

Kukulkán loved the Mayan people.

He wanted them to have their
own paradise on Earth.

He had been especially happy
when he gave them maize.

He taught the people to
plant the corn seeds.

He taught them to pick the crop
when it was ripe.

The Maya learned from
Kukulkán how to mash the corn and
flatten it into tasty tortillas.

Maize became their most important crop.

Kukulkán gave the Maya everything
they needed for a happy life.
He gave them books to read.
He gave them a calendar to keep track
of the seasons and the stars.
He gave the people music,
and he taught them how to sing and dance.

The Mayan people built a stone temple to show
Kukulkán they were grateful for his gifts.
They built it in the middle of
their jungle city, Chichén Itzá.
The temple was shaped like a pyramid.
It had ninety-one steps.
The steps were steep, like a ladder to the sky.
On the top was a stone house.
It faced the morning star.
It became Kukulkán's home on Earth.

Every day, the Maya worked and
played and sang.
They knew that each dawn,
when they saw the morning star,
Kukulkán would come down from the
temple to watch over his people.
What a wonderful life the Maya had
in the green jungle with Kukulkán
as their leader!

Jaguar Nights

But every happy story has a dark side too.

And now it is time for you to meet Night Jaguar.

He too was a god from paradise.

He and Kukulkán were twin brothers.

But they were as different as night and day.

Kukulkán, like the daylight,

was warm and friendly.

Jaguar, like the night,

was cool and fearsome.

Night Jaguar shared his

brother's temple in Chichén Itzá.

When the evening star shone, Night Jaguar

kept watch from the temple.

At the end of each day, the Maya
stopped their work on the milpas.
They headed back to their *nahs*,
their little homes.
Night Jaguar ruled the night.
His job was to put the sun to bed and to
protect the city during the dark nights.
He did not wear a cloak
of beautiful feathers.

Some people say he wore jaguar fur.

Others say he was a real jaguar.

He was fierce and very good at his job.

Every night, when the people were sleeping,

he crept out his doorway.

He prowled the streets,

passing palaces and temples.

He studied the Mayan carvings of the stars.

He stalked the empty marketplace.

At night, the city was very quiet.
The only sound was the rustle
of palm trees in the moonlight.
"I am the Night Jaguar,"
he announced to the sky.
But who was listening?
Birds slept.
People snored.
Children dreamed in their beds.
As Night Jaguar prowled, he thought.
Why did the Maya deserve the gifts
of music and corn and books?
He believed the gods should keep
the best treasures in paradise.
Otherwise, the Maya might become
as great as the gods.

Maybe he was selfish.

Maybe he was not the giving type.

Maybe he thought his brother had
already given the Maya too much.
Still, Night Jaguar guarded
the city every night.
When the sun rose, he crept
up the temple steps until the
evening star shone again.

As Night Jaguar rested,
he smiled a secret grin.
I know one thing the Maya
will never have, he thought.
And what was that?
Chocolate, the gods' favorite food.

Flying to Paradise

Dawn came.

Kukulkán woke to the singing sound

of his people's voices.

Heaps of fruit sat at his doorstep.

Bundles of vegetables sat next to the fruit.

Clay pots and woven baskets held the food.

These were gifts from the hardworking

Mayan people.

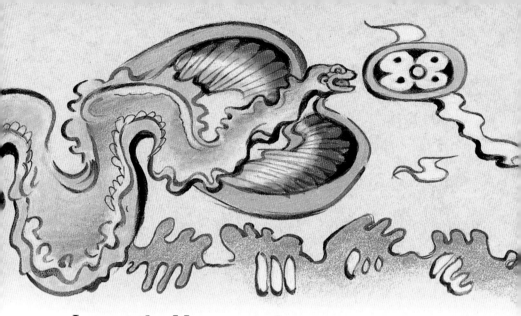

I want the Mayans to have
something special, he thought.
Kukulkán knew he must return
to paradise for this special gift.
The task would not be easy.
He knew Night Jaguar would not be happy.
Kukulkán would have to sneak off
while his brother was sleeping.
When the sun was high in the sky,
he spread his mighty wings.
Off he flew to paradise.

He arrived just in time for a fancy dinner.

Music played.

Banana trees swayed in the breeze.

Kukulkán strolled past the butterflies and
through the gardens.

Nearly all of his family sat at the table.

They welcomed him.

More than one hundred gods
had come to the dinner.

On his right was the goddess of the moon.

To his left was the god Chac.

Chac ruled the rain.

The gods feasted on papayas,

mangoes, and melons.

They ate tall stacks of corn tortillas.

They poured cup after cup of foamy

chocolate, called *chocolatl*.

The gods had honey to sweeten

the chocolate.

They used chilies to spice it up.

Kukulkán finally decided to speak.
"The Maya are good people, and they
deserve a special gift," he said.
"I want to bring them …"
Suddenly all the gods became silent.
Everyone stopped eating.
They set down their jade goblets.
They listened.

"I want to bring them … a chocolate tree,"
said Kukulkán boldly.

Instantly, there was an uproar.

Gods began shouting.

Goddesses argued.

"He wants to share our finest treasure
with the Maya?" asked one.

"Then the Maya will have everything we
gods in paradise have," said Chac.

"I think it's only fair," said another.

Kukulkán stood and left the table.

He went into the garden,

away from the noise.

He sat beneath a cacao tree to think.

Chocolate will bring the people happiness,

he thought.

My happy people will grow wise

and create a paradise on Earth.

Yet was it right to share this treasure

of the gods?

Kukulkán pondered the question.

Hundreds of cacao trees grew in paradise.

Every tree had many pods.

Every pod had nearly 60 seeds inside.

Why not share the wealth? he decided.

The gods shuffled off to bed, grumbling.

Some agreed with Kukulkán.

Some thought it was a terrible idea.

But Kukulkán had made up his mind.

He waited until everyone was sleeping.

Then he found a small cacao tree.

It was loaded with red pods.

He snatched the tree up, roots and all.

He looked around to be sure
no one was watching.

Then he raced through the garden,
past the waterfalls.

He flew up a rainbow.

He jumped onto the morning star.

WHOOSH! The star sped him back to Earth.

Trouble in the Temple

Night Jaguar saw the morning star

appear in the sky above Chichén Itzá.

He dashed to the top of the pyramid.

He hid in the shadows.

He knew his brother had been to paradise.

He was suspicious.

As Kukulkán flew down to his temple,
Night Jaguar watched.
He saw something beneath his brother's robe
of quetzal feathers.
What was it?
Kukulkán stood atop the temple and
sang to summon the Mayan people.
Children and men and women came hurrying.
They surrounded the temple.

"My people," said Kukulkán.

His voice was magic.

It carried far into the jungle.

From beneath his feathered cloak,

he pulled out the tree.

He lifted it above his head.

"What is it?" everyone asked.

"It is a cacao tree!" Kukulkán said.

Kukulkán came down the steps

to show his new treasure.

From deep in the shadows,

Night Jaguar growled.

He paced back and forth, fuming.

How dare his brother bring the gods'

favorite food to these people!

Down below, the Maya were excited.

Kukulkán pulled a red pod off the tree.
With a knife, he whacked it in half.
It was full of seeds that looked like
white almonds.

The people knew that corn grew
from hard, yellow seeds.
Avocados grew from big, round seeds.
Papayas grew from slippery, black seeds.
So what would grow from these soft,
pale seeds?

"Chocolate," said Kukulkán.
"The beans make the most delicious
drink you can imagine."
He showed the people how to plant
the seeds.
They needed a place with both
a little shade and a little sun.
"The trees will grow quickly,"
he said to the Maya.
"And then, I will show you how to make
chocolatl, the drink of the gods."

Kukulkán heard a snarl from the temple.

He strode up the steep steps.

He needed to make peace

with his brother about the gift.

But when he got to the top of the temple,

Night Jaguar was gone.

He had already leaped away

into the thick jungle.

Chocolate for Everyone

Kukulkán sighed.

He knew exactly what Night Jaguar
was planning.

He would tell the gods that
Kukulkán had stolen the cacao tree.

What would happen when they found out?

Suddenly, the sky grew dark.

Thunder boomed.

Bolts of lightning slashed the fields.

The people ran for shelter.

Kukulkán stood atop his
Chichén Itzá temple.

He heard the anger in the thunder.

It came from paradise.

The gods knew.

Now the Maya had the gods' favorite food.

They would plant many chocolate trees.

They would carry the seeds from
the fruit to the north,
the south, the east, and the west.

Earth would become a paradise.

"Kukulkán!" roared the gods' voices.

"We are outraged!

You will never, ever set foot in
paradise again!"

And so, Kukulkán did not return
to paradise.

At harvesttime, he taught his people to
gather the cacao seeds.

Some would grow new trees.

Others would be used to make chocolate.

Kukulkán showed them how to dry
the beans in the sun and to roast them
over a fire.
He taught them to use a metate—a stone—
to grind the beans with maize into a powder.
He celebrated with his people when they
drank chocolate for the first time.

Mayan families were soon drinking
chocolatl at every meal.
Cacao seeds spread far and wide.
People all across Earth
discovered chocolate.
Thanks to chocolate, the world
is a sweeter place.

So the next time you have a sip
of warm cocoa, a bite of fudge brownie,
or a spoonful of chocolate ice cream,
just think how lucky you are.
Think of Kukulkán riding to Earth
on the morning star to bring chocolate
to the Mayan people.

Authors' Note

Many people in Mexico know the tale of Kukulkán, the feathered serpent who stole a chocolate tree from paradise. Legend says Kukulkán traveled on the morning star to bring cacao to his people. His actions angered the gods, and they banished him from paradise forever.

The story of Kukulkán comes from the Maya, Aztec, and Toltec cultures. Different communities tell the story in different ways—but in every case, the tale is brief. We are left to fill in the details. And so we have. We incorporated some history of the ancient Mayan lifestyle and culture into the chocolate tree story.

The stories of Kukulkán ("Quetzalcoatl" to the Aztecs) are mystical, complicated, and contradictory. In our tale, we introduced the Mayan god Night Jaguar as an antagonist. Called Xólotl (SHO-lotel), this jaguar was often represented as the evil twin brother of Kukulkán or as the dark side of Kukulkán himself. Xólotl, a shape-shifter, appears in various stories as a jaguar, a dog, a skeleton, or a monster animal. This fearsome god is the perfect counterpoint to the generous Kukulkán. We also presented paradise as a place with ample desserts and other treats—a contrast to the earthly world, where the Mayans had to work hard to grow the food they ate.

Chichén Itzá, one of the most important Mayan cities, sits on the Yucatán Peninsula of Mexico. On July 7th, 2007, the New Open World Corporation in Switzerland announced that voters had chosen Chichén Itzá as one of the New Seven Wonders of the World. The city is also a UNESCO World Heritage Site, and its centerpiece is Kukulkán's temple. At the spring and fall equinox, sunlight shining on the pyramid's north staircase creates a shape that looks like a serpent—Kukulkán.

Further Reading and Websites

Nelson, Robin. *From Cocoa Bean to Chocolate*. Minneapolis: Lerner Publications Company, 2003. Read all about how cocoa beans are made into a delicious treat.

Rockwell, Anne. *The Boy Who Wouldn't Obey: A Mayan Legend*. New York: Greenwillow Books, 2000. The Mayan rain god comes to Earth to find a boy to be his servant—but the boy causes big trouble for the mighty god!

Sepehri, Sandy. *How the Peacock Got His Feathers*. Vero Beach, FL: Rourke Publishing, 2007. Based on a Mayan legend, this story explains the origins of the peacock's beautiful feathers.

Takacs, Stefanie. *The Maya*. New York: Children's Press, 2003. Read all about the Mayans' land, daily life, and beliefs.

Wisniewski, David. *Rain Player*. New York: Clarion Books, 1991. The stakes are high when young Pik challenges the rain god to a game of *pok-a-tok*. Can Pik win, or will the rain god prevail?

American Folklore
http://www.americanfolklore.net
This site includes a variety of folktales, including stories from Mexican and Native American cultures.

Mayan Kids
http://www.mayankids.com
Visit this site to read interesting facts about Mayan people, places, and beliefs. You will also find a helpful glossary and fun games you can play.

Glossary

cacao (kuh-COW): the tree on which cacao fruits grow. Inside the fruits are cacao seeds, which are used to make chocolate.

Chac (CHAHK): the Mayan god of rain

Chichén Itzá (chee-CHEN-eet-ZAH): an ancient Mayan city in the state of Yucatán, Mexico

chocolatl (chaw-koh-LOH-tuhl): a Mayan word that gave us the English word *chocolate*. Chocolatl is also the Mayan word for the drink we call cocoa—but chocolatl is different from the cocoa we know. Mayans didn't use milk in their chocolatl, and they flavored it with honey and chilies.

cocoa: a drink made from milk, sugar, and the ground-up seeds, or beans, of the cacao tree

jade: a mineral the Maya used to make jewelry and carved artifacts, such as cups and masks. Mayan jade is a rich green color.

Kukulkán (coo-cool-KAHN): an ancient Mayan god and king. *Feathered Serpent* is another name for Kukulkán.

maize (MAZE): corn

Maya (MY-uh): people of the Yucatán, both ancient and modern

metate (muh-TAH-tee): a stone slab used to grind corn, grains, and dried cacao seeds

milpas (MILL-pahs): family farms where the Maya grew corn, beans, squash, and sweet potatoes

nahs (NAHS): Mayan houses

quetzal (ket-SAL): a rain forest bird with very long tail feathers. Quetzals are green, blue, gold, and red.

tortillas (tor-TEE-yuhs): thin, flat bread made from corn